my little Pony™

Crystal Princess

The Runaway Rainbow

The unicorns were busy preparing for the Rainbow Celebration
in Unicornia. Princess Rarity had a starring role—
with a magic wand, she would help make the first rainbow
of the season! She just had to learn how.
"Rarity! Please pay attention!" her teacher, Cheerilee, said.

Rarity wasn't very interested in the lessons,
but she did like twirling the magic wand.
Rarity waved the wand above her head.
"Be careful!" cried Cheerilee, but it was too late.
In a flash of sparks, Rarity was gone!

Thump! The Breezies were quite surprised when Rarity
dropped out of nowhere. "Welcome to Breezie Blossom!"
said Tra-La-La. "What's that bump on your head?"
"That's not a bump," said Rarity. "That's my horn! I'm a unicorn."
Rarity explained what happened.

"Maybe the ponies will know what to do," said Zipzee.
"We'll take you with us to the Ponyville Rainbow Celebration."
"But I make the first rainbow of the season," said Rarity.
"If I'm not back in Unicornia in time, there won't be
any rainbows anywhere, even in Ponyville."

Rarity followed her new friends to Ponyville.
"Welcome, Breezies!" said Rainbow Dash.
"Who is your new friend?"
"That's Rarity. She fell out of the sky!" Tra-La-La explained.
"And she makes rainbows with a magic wand."

"I'm from Unicornia," Rarity said. "I must get back home for
the Rainbow Celebration there. Do you know the way?"
"I've never heard of Unicornia, but maybe Spike has,"
said Rainbow Dash. "Follow me!"

The ponies and Rarity went to visit Spike, the wise little dragon.
Reading from a big book, Spike told a story about unicorns
and how they make the rainbows that brighten the skies
over Ponyville and everywhere else.

"You are a very special unicorn, Rarity," said Spike.
"If we don't get you back to Unicornia,
there won't be any rainbows this season."
"No rainbows?" cried Rainbow Dash.
"We have to bring Rarity home!"

The group set out on the journey. Over mountains,
across fields, and past rivers, the travelers walked on and on.
Minty noticed that the pretty colors in Rainbow Dash's
hair were starting to fade. They had to hurry!

"Oh, no!" Rarity whispered. "What if we don't get back in time? If there are no rainbows this year, it will be all my fault!" Rarity shook everyone awake. "We have to keep going!" she said.

As the tired group trudged along in the dark,
Rarity heard a rustle in the bushes. It was Cheerilee!
Rarity had never been happier. All she wanted was to go home.

Cheerilee was relieved to see that Rarity still had her magic wand.
As Rarity's old and new friends looked on, she waved the wand in
the special Princess Twirl to call the Crystal Carriage.
Everyone climbed in for a ride through the sky to Unicornia.

Time was running out for Rarity to make the first rainbow.
As soon as the carriage landed, the unicorns ran to the castle.
All across the land, rainbow-striped colors were fading.
They had to make the rainbow—fast!

"Oh, no!" cried Cheerilee.

"The rainbow colors are gone. We've lost our chance."

Rarity looked around at the dull room full of sad faces.

She knew she had to do something.

"We have to try," she said. "We can't just give up."

The unicorns put their horns together.

At first, nothing happened.

Suddenly, Rarity's pink horn grew longer and started to glow.

Then Cheerilee's purple horn began to glow, too.

"It's working!" cried Rainbow Dash. A flash of light from the
unicorns' horns flew up to the ceiling and through the castle dome!

Ribbons of color filled the sky.
They raced around Unicornia and out over the land,
even as far as Ponyville.

As all the beautiful colors returned, Cheerilee told Rarity,
"You are a true unicorn princess." Everyone clapped and cheered.

"I couldn't have done it without all of you," said Rarity.
"I promise that, for as long as I am Princess, there will be
rainbows every day as a gift for my wonderful friends!"

This book belongs to:

_____

And her ponies:

_____

_____

My Little Pony Crystal Princess: *The Runaway Rainbow*
Text and illustrations © 2006 Hasbro, Inc.
HASBRO and its logo and MY LITTLE PONY and all related characters
are trademarks of Hasbro and are used with permission.
© 2006 Hasbro. All Rights Reserved.
HarperCollins®, 🍃®, and HarperFestival® are trademarks of HarperCollins Publishers.
For more information address HarperCollins Children's Books, a division of HarperCollins Publishers,
1350 Avenue of the Americas, New York, NY 10019.
Printed in the U.S.A.
Library of Congress catalog card number: 2006923364
Designed by John Sazaklis

US $3.99 / $4.99 CAN
ISBN-13: 978-0-06-111693-3
ISBN-10: 0-06-111693-9
9 780061 116933
50399

my little Pony™

crystal Princess The Runaway Rainbow

Based on the animated movie!

DB86507378